For all those who love books
A story to touch the heart.

92
Co

D0890162

The Man Who Loved Books

The Man Who Loved Books

by

Jean Fritz

illuminated by

Trina Schart Hyman

G.P. Putnam's Sons · New York

Text copyright © 1981 by Jean Fritz.
Illustrations copyright © 1981 by Trina Schart Hyman.
All rights reserved. Published simultaneously in Canada
by Academic Press Canada Limited, Toronto.
Printed in the United States of America.
First impression.
Library of Congress Cataloging in Publication Data
Fritz, Jean.
The man who loved books.
Summary: A brief biography of the Irish saint who was
known for his love of books and his missionary work
throughout Scotland.
1. Columba, Saint, 521-597—Juvenile literature.
2. Christian saints—Ireland—Biography—Juvenile literature.
[1. Columba, Saint, 521-597. 2. Saints.
3. Books and reading—History.]
I. Hyman, Trina Schart. II. Title.
BX4700.C7F74 1981 270.2'092'4 [B] 80-12614
ISBN 0-399-20715-5

To
BILL and Bea

J.F.

For my friend
Tomie

T.S.H.

ONG AGO in Ireland there lived a man named Columba who loved books. In fact, he was wild for books, but books were still such a new thing in Ireland, they were hard to come by. If someone wanted to read a new book, he might have to walk the length of the land just to find one. If he wanted to own the book, he would have to copy it by hand.

Now if it had been just stories that Columba had wanted, he would have had no trouble. Traveling bands of storytelling poets (bards they were called) were forever stopping by to tell stories. They were grand old stories, memorized word for word and passed down through the years. After the telling, the bards would jingle a gold bowl that hung by chains from the tips of their spears. They would jingle the bowl right under the noses of their listeners who were supposed to drop coins into it. If they dropped enough coins, the bards would put their names into fine songs of praise. But if they were stingy, the bards would make up mean songs about their stinginess and sing them over the land. So of course people tried to keep on the good side of bards.

Columba loved the old stories and because he was the son of a chieftain, he had even studied under a famous bard. But once he had learned to read, nothing took the place of books.

He had learned early. When he was still a young boy, a prophet, studying the stars one night, had seen a message cast in the sky. Columba should read, the prophet said. He should begin now. And so the letters of the alphabet had been baked inside a cake and Columba had eaten the cake. Once the letters were digested he began practicing, and before long he was writing words on a wax slate and reading them too. Only a few people could read in Columba's day and many didn't go along with the idea of reading at all. If a person could read, they said, what would happen to memory? Why remember stories when they could be set down in books? Who would need bards? But Columba said there was room enough in Ireland for both bards and books. And both should be honored.

COLUMBA GREW to be a great giant of a man with a grand voice that could be heard a mile away and whatever he did, he did totally. Whatever he loved, he loved with all his heart. In addition to books, Columba loved Ireland. Every green blade of Irish grass. Every square inch of Irish sod. And he loved the church. To show how much he loved it, Columba gave up worldly ways. He put on a prickly, rough shirt made out of the manes of horses and wore it next to his skin. He slept with a stone for a pillow.

But neither Ireland nor the church came in the way of Columba's love of books. He was determined to read every book in Ireland and to copy every one that he read. Since books were generally kept in monasteries, Columba spent much of his time walking from one monastery to another. The trouble was that monks in monasteries were sometimes jealous of their books. They liked having an only copy and when they saw Columba striding down the road, they would give the alarm. "Quick, hide the new books," they would say. And when Columba arrived, they would shake their heads sadly. "No, no new books here."

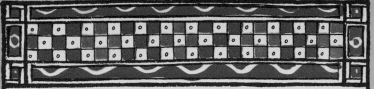

One day Columba heard that a hermit named Longarad-of-the-Hairy-Legs had a book that Columba had never seen. So of course Columba called on the hermit right away. Yes, Longarad-of-the-Hairy-Legs said, he did have that book, but he would not let Columba see it. No matter how much Columba pleaded, he would not. No, he would not. No, no, and no again. By this time Columba's anger was red-hot, reaching right to the roots of his hair.

"May thy books no longer do thee any good!" he cried. And off he stamped, his shirt prickling as he went.

Another time Columba's good friend Finian came back from a trip to Rome with a new book. Since Finian was a friend, Columba set off in high spirits with his inks and his pens and his parchment in his satchel. For company, he took with him his pet crane.

Finian welcomed Columba to his monastery and said, of course, he could look at the book. But he must not copy it.

That night Columba and his crane went into the library where the book was kept on the end of a chain locked into a stone wall. Carefully Columba opened the book. And heaven be praised, what a book it was! Great capital letters with fishes and flowers nestled in them. Spiraling circles spilling into margins. And small letters, round and black and bold, sitting side by side in friendship like fat little birds on a line.

"Ah, Crane," Columba whispered, "what a beauty it is! What a beauty!"

The next night after everyone in the monastery was asleep, Columba crept to the library with his pens and his parchment and began copying the book. The next night too. And the next and the next. He had no time for the great capital letters or the spiraling circles, but he did get the words down until there was only one night's work left to do.

And that night Finian became suspicious. He sent a messenger to the library and, of course, what the messenger found was not one book but two, with Columba in the candlelight between them. So a great argument arose. Finian said that he had not given permission for his book to be copied, so the copied book belonged to him. Columba said that since he had copied it, the book was his. Neither man would give an inch and so they went to the High King of Ireland to let him judge.

Together they stood before the High King, first one giving his arguments and then the other.

The High King bent his head to the left and bent it to the right, weighing the matter between the two men.

Then he ruled in favor of Finian. "To every cow belongs her calf," he said, "and to every book its son-book."

Columba's anger blazed. "It is a wrong judgment," he cried, "and I shall be avenged."

Straightaway Columba took off for the mountains where his kinfolk lived. His father had many warriors in his service, none of them backward about making war. No sooner had Columba told his story than the men were off marching to meet the army of the High King. Columba went along and prayed. And whether it was the prayers or the fighting that won the battle—who can say? But in the end the High King was defeated in a terrible defeat. Three thousand men lay dead on his side and one man dead on Columba's. So for certain, Columba was avenged.

Yet he did not feel like a victor. Now that it was over, he felt miserable inside his prickly shirt. Three thousand and one men who had been alive yesterday were dead today, and all because of one book. Columba had behaved like a man of the world, not like a man of the church, and he was ashamed. He would have to punish himself with the worst punishment he could think of. So he vowed to leave Ireland and never set eyes on it again.

SADLY COLUMBA said good-bye to his friends, to his beloved homeland, and to the book he had copied—the cause of his woe. Then he climbed into his boat, *Dewy Red,* and with twelve companions and his pet crane he set sail north for an unknown island to take his punishment.

There were plenty of islands to pick from. Columba stopped first at one, then another, but each time that he looked south, he could still see Ireland. Once he thought he'd gone far enough, but when he climbed a hill, there was Ireland, green as ever, in the distance. But at last Columba came to the island of Iona. He climbed to the top of the highest hill, squinted south, and when all he could see was sea and surf, he knew he'd found his new home.

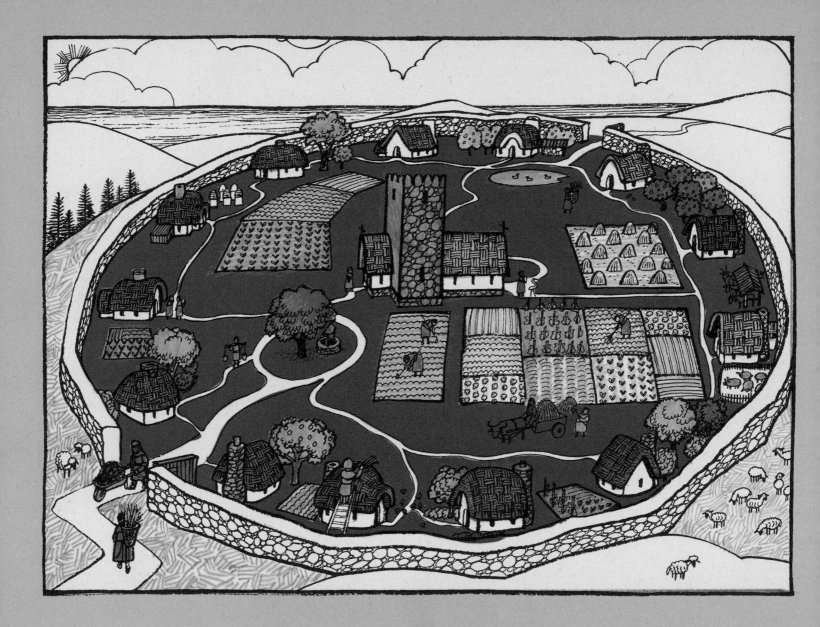

Columba and his friends built a church and around it thirteen huts (one for each man), and around the huts a wall. This was his town and the people were his family. As time went on more people joined his family, for Columba was quick to make friends not only with his neighbors but also with people from nearby islands and even those from the mainland of Scotland lying to the east. All through the north he traveled, preaching and starting small churches as he went. Once he walked across the whole width of Scotland and persuaded the king himself to become a Christian.

Of course Columba was homesick for Ireland. There was not a bird which flew south that he did not envy its going. And of course he missed the joy of new books. Still he had the Bible, the most important book, and he was determined that every church should have its own copy. So night after night he lined up the letters, round and black and bold, and before he was through, he had made three hundred copies of the New Testament in his own hand.

COLUMBA WAS seventy years old and had lived on Iona for twenty-eight years when one day a fleet of boats from Ireland sailed into the harbor. Columba rushed down to the shore to welcome them. Twenty bishops were on board, forty priests, and thirty deacons. Ninety men in all and every one Irish! Columba could not go quickly enough from one to another.

They had come, the bishops explained, because there was trouble at home. It was the bards. They had become so greedy, they weren't content with coins any longer. They had even commanded a king to give them his royal brooch. And if he refused, the bards had threatened to sing songs that would disgrace the king before his kingdom. Now a great meeting had been called, and all bards were to be banished from the country.

Listening to the bishops, Columba was like a man whipped by winds. How could the bards behave so badly? But banished! How could Ireland get along without its bards? What kind of people would the Irish become without stories and songs to liven them? It was unthinkable.

"Then come back with us," the bishops and the priests and the deacons begged.

"Speak at the meeting. Only you can make the kings and bards listen."

But how could Columba go when he had vowed not to set eyes on Ireland again?

Yet how could he not go?

Night after night, Columba lay awake, setting the vow against the stories and the stories against the vow.

At last he found an answer. He had never vowed not to set foot on Ireland, had he? It was only his eyes he had punished. So he tied a blindfold over his eyes and sailed back to Ireland with the bishops and the priests and the deacons. He took his place in the prow of the first boat, for though he couldn't see, he wanted to feel himself drawing closer to Ireland.

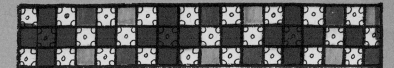

The meeting had already assembled when Columba arrived. All the local kings of Ireland were there, all the nobles, all the churchmen, and twelve hundred bards. When they saw Columba, blindfolded, being led before them, they rose in his honor. And when Columba began to speak, they smiled at each other. For neither the blindfold nor the years had made a difference in that wonderful voice. Nor in the speech. For who but Columba could find words that would set the bards and the kings both at ease?

By the end of the meeting the bards had agreed to rules that would keep them in order. And the kings had agreed to let the bards stay.

Then Columba went back to Iona, his homesickness healed like a scab over a sore. For hadn't he felt the good Irish sod once again under his feet? Hadn't he smelled the green smell of the land? Hadn't he heard the fine Irish voices of the bards singing the old songs?

And now he was in haste to get back to his island and take off his blindfold. For in his satchel he had a new book that the bishops had given him. A fine fat book, it felt. A feast, surely.

Columba lived for six more years, happy with his family and his work. When he died, he was doing what he liked best. He had his parchments, his pens, and his inks before him. He died in the middle of copying a sentence.

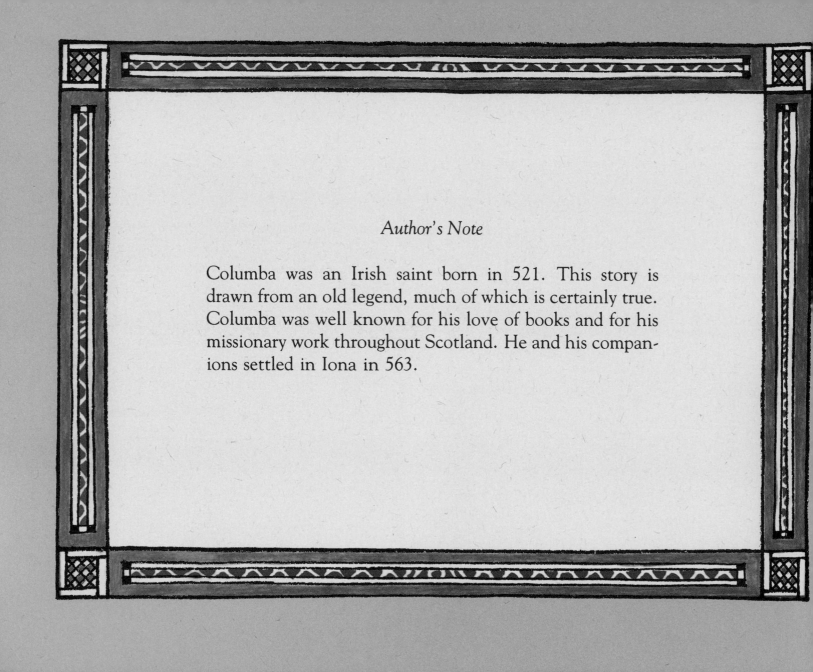

Author's Note

Columba was an Irish saint born in 521. This story is drawn from an old legend, much of which is certainly true. Columba was well known for his love of books and for his missionary work throughout Scotland. He and his companions settled in Iona in 563.